LINDA WALVOORD GIRARD

Alex, the Kid with AIDS

Illustrations by BLANCHE SIMS

ALBERT WHITMAN & COMPANY • Morton Grove, Illinois

The author wishes to thank the following people, who have generously provided information: David Martin, M.D., of Traverse City, Michigan, a specialist in pediatric infectious diseases; Donna Harris, M.S., R.N., of Children's Memorial Hospital, Chicago, Illinois; Barbara Abel, R.N., a school nurse in Moraga, California; Bernard Wiegand, M.D., of Orinda, California; Rita Fahrner, R.N., Coordinator for the HIV/AIDS Programs, Children's Hospital, Oakland, California; and Paul G. Nilsen, principal of Central School in Wilmette, Illinois, whose staff and board carried out an inspiring model of community education when a student was diagnosed as having AIDS.

Library of Congress Cataloging-in-Publication Data

Girard, Linda Walvoord.
Alex, the kid with AIDS/Linda Walvoord Girard;
illustrated by Blanche Sims.
p.   cm.
Summary: Alex, a fourth grader with AIDS, makes a
new friend and learns that although he is sick, he
can't misbehave in school.
ISBN: 0-8075-0245-6 (hardcover)
ISBN: 0-8075-0247-2 (paperback)
[1. AIDS (Disease)—Fiction. 2. Behavior—Fiction.
3. Schools—Fiction. 4. Friendship—Fiction.]
I. Sims, Blanche, ill.
II. Title.
PZ7.G43953 A1   1991   89-77592
[Fic]—dc20   CIP
                                                AC

The text typeface is Souvenir Light.
The illustrations are in watercolor and ink.

The day I started fourth grade, I never dreamed how much trouble I'd get into, and all because of Alex, the kid with AIDS.

Alex walked into our class three days late. He stood there in a blue sweater, looking shy, while our teacher introduced him. She told him to sit in the empty seat, next to me. Alex sat down without looking at anyone. The kids were quiet.

We'd all heard about Alex. Ever since the summer, when his family first moved here, some people had been whispering that Alex had AIDS. He'd gotten it from a blood transfusion. Finally, his parents decided it was too hard to keep a secret. Now everybody knew.

In August, the school had sent out a letter saying there would be a student with AIDS. The letter was signed by the principal and a doctor. They said it would be safe to go to school with this kid and to play with him.

When school began, the nurse came around to tell us about AIDS and let us know Alex would be in *our* class. I wasn't afraid to be near Alex, but I still didn't like being the one to sit next to him. I felt embarrassed. And I felt stuck.

At first, our teacher, Mrs. Timmers, didn't call on Alex. On his second day, I saw him sneak a video game into his desk. He'd pull it out sometimes and play with it. It made soft beeps. Mrs. Timmers looked right at him a few times, but she didn't say anything.

At recess, Alex didn't ask to play ball, and nobody asked him. He'd sit by himself on the bench or on the swings. I thought he looked sad, but I always forgot about him.

My best friends were Roger and Frank. If football got boring, we'd pick on Louise for fun, as usual. Louise has been in my class since kindergarten. We like to bug each other.

One day Roger, Frank, and I yelled an old rhyme at her:

> Louise, Louise, big and fat—
> can't tell where her feet are at.
> When she skip ropes on the ground,
> the earth will shake for miles around!

"Shut up, Mosquito Brain!" screamed Louise. She's not fat—that's just how the rhyme goes. But she got mad anyhow.

"Louise, don't yell!" shouted Mrs. Zanes, the playground supervisor. She's so strict she makes kids miss recess if they don't play right. She lets boys yell, but not girls. Frank calls her "Dragon Lady" because she's really tall and wears a green jacket. Luckily, Mrs. Zanes hadn't heard our song.

On the way into school, Frank and I told Louise she had legs like an elephant and she should go to the zoo and not come back. "Well, in that case," she said, and WHAM! She kicked my shins. "Try an elephant kick!"

I shoved Louise against the coatrack, and it clanged like a big gong. Mrs. Zanes came running in.

"What's going on in here?" she snapped.

"Louise kicked me!"

"He called me names!"

"Mrs. Timmers will hear about this," Mrs. Zanes said.

"I'll get you, Turkey!" Louise whispered to me.

"Try!" I whispered back.

During afternoon recess, Mrs. Timmers made us write, "I will not create disturbances" one hundred times. That's four whole sheets of paper each, if you write small.

Alex happened to be there, too, for help with spelling.

"Pen-nant," Mrs. Timmers said, sounding out the word.

"P-E-N-N-E-N-T," Alex spelled.

"No, Alex, it's A-N-T," she said.

"Oh, yeah," said Alex. He had missed the first days of school, when we had that word.

I kept writing sentences. *I will not create disturbances.*

"Could Michael study with me?" Alex asked.

"Good idea, Alex," said Mrs. Timmers. "Michael, you may be excused from the rest of your sentences. Instead, review spelling with Alex."

I helped Alex for about fifteen minutes. While we worked, he picked up a paper, wrote on it, and passed it back. He had printed six times, "I will always tease Louise."

I never knew Alex was funny! We giggled.

"Boys, get to work," Mrs. Timmers said.

We slipped the paper into Louise's math book and finished the spelling quietly. Louise had to finish *her* sentences. When we left, I made a face at her. She looked real mad.

The second week of October, Mrs. Timmers announced we all had to write poems. The PTA was giving a twenty-dollar prize for the best poem in each grade. She put us in pairs.

I was hoping for Frank. I got Alex.

Mrs. Timmers talked a long time about how to write poems. She said we could each write our own or work with our partner.

"I hate poems," I told Alex.

"That's okay. We can do it together," he said. "I've got an idea."

> Mrs. Zanes
>
> lost her brains

he penned in neat letters, skipping a line in between just like Mrs. Timmers said.

I laughed. "Alex, you'd better watch it," I told him.

"Naw, I can write any poem I want because I'm sick," Alex said. He was chewing his pencil and running his hand through his red hair.

I just looked at him. How could he talk about AIDS like that, as if it were the measles?

Alex wrote some more:

> They weren't found

He stopped to think. "On the ground!" I whispered, and Alex added it. We kept going.

Alex printed our names on top of the paper. I gave the poem a title: "DRAGON LADY." Alex added, "Poetry Contest, October 12, Room 4B."

Dragon Lady

Alex Larson
Michael Reynolds
Poetry Contest
October 12, Room 4B

Mrs. Zanes

lost her brains.

They weren't found

on the ground.

She bought some more

at the store.

But they didn't fit,

come to think of it.

No brains, no brains.

Poor Mrs. Zanes!

"Are you sure we can put a poem about a teacher in the contest?" I asked him again.

"I told you I can. I'm sick."

Alex was probably right, I thought. The PTA would feel sorry for him. Anyhow, *I* knew the poem was awesome. We were going to win ten dollars each—if Mrs. Zanes wasn't around. I figured all the other kids were writing boring poems about clouds or daffodils. I noticed Louise's paper was still blank. She peered over at us, but I didn't let her see our poem.

"How come you're so good at writing poems when you're a crummy speller?" I asked Alex.

"I'm not a crummy speller if I learn the words," he said. He pulled out a comic book and started reading even though Mrs. Timmers was looking straight at us.

I was admiring our poem when Louise came by my desk, pretending to be on her way to the bathroom. She ripped it right out of my hands. She was down the aisle before I could even get up.

"I hate Louise!" I said to Alex.

"It's okay," he said. "I can write the poem over." He almost finished, but then we had math, so he stuck the poem in his desk.

The next day, Alex was absent. While he was gone, the nurse came and gave us a talk. She said, "I'd like to remind you children of some important things."

The nurse said you can't catch AIDS by being around someone with the disease. Alex could cough on kids, but they wouldn't get AIDS. Even if he threw up on someone, that person wouldn't get AIDS. The only way we could get AIDS from Alex was to have his blood get into our blood. So there was one rule we had to follow. If Alex got a nosebleed or a cut, we had to be extra careful not to touch the blood in case we had a scratch or cut, too. A teacher or the nurse would clean the blood up.

"Yuk," said Louise under her breath.

"Quiet, Birdbrain," I said. Big-mouth Louise. Alex wasn't my friend or anything, but she didn't have to act mean.

"Where did Alex go today?" asked Martha.

"He's at the hospital, getting a treatment," said the nurse.

"Is Alex going to die?" asked Roger.

"Alex has a serious illness," the nurse said, "but we hope he will live a long time. Some people with AIDS do."

"Maybe he'll just get over it. I get over my colds," said Jane.

"AIDS isn't like a cold," said the nurse. "The body can't get rid of the virus that causes the disease. But doctors are working hard to find a cure."

I looked at the bright maple trees outside, and the blue sky. I wondered if Alex thought about dying. He looked okay in school, so it didn't *seem* like he was in big trouble.

Alex was kind of nice—he was really funny, and he helped me when I couldn't write a poem. I felt sorry he had to be sick.

That afternoon, Mrs. Timmers reminded us our contest poems were due. Ours wasn't finished! I fished the poem out of Alex's desk, shoving aside the comic books and the video game. He hadn't copied over the last two lines. I racked my brains and finally remembered the words.

Right before recess, I gave Mrs. Timmers our poem. It was a little crumpled, and I didn't have the same color pen as Alex had used.

"This isn't very neat, Michael," she said, as she slipped the poem into her folder.

"We did it right the first time, but Louise stole our poem," I said. "We had to start over."

"It's still messy," she said.

During recess, I saw Louise hand a paper to Mrs. Zanes.

It was almost time to go home when Mrs. Zanes came charging into our room with a folder in her hand. She slammed the door behind her and glared at the class. Then she whispered to Mrs. Timmers, who nodded. I had a sinking feeling. Finally Mrs. Timmers took the folder, and Dragon Lady stalked out the door. She slammed it again.

After the bell rang, Mrs. Timmers called me to her desk. She said Alex and I had to see her, tomorrow.

I called Alex that night. "Alex, we're in trouble. Louise gave our poem to Mrs. Zanes!"

But Alex wasn't upset. "I showed the poem to the doctor. He said it was good. It'll win."

"Yeah, but the doctor doesn't know Mrs. Zanes," I said.

I stayed awake really late, worrying. Last time I got into trouble at school, my parents grounded me for a whole week!

When we came in the next morning, Mrs. Timmers said the class was going to the library for a talk on biographies. As Alex and I got up, we glanced at each other. Hey, maybe she forgot!

"All of you except Michael and Alex," she added.

We sat back down. My heart was pounding.

"No sweat," Alex whispered. "I can get us out of this." The class left, and the room was quiet.

"Alex," Mrs. Timmers said as she looked over her glasses, "you have a little problem, and I *don't* mean your illness."

Alex was so surprised that he dropped his pencil.

"I've been taking it easy with you, treating you like somebody from outer space," she said. "I made a mistake, Alex. You read comic books. You play with your video game in your desk. And now this poem. If it's not okay for somebody else to write this poem and turn it in, then it's not okay for you. And Michael, you should have known better, too."

Alex's cheeks were red. "I'm sorry," he mumbled.

"Me, too," I said.

Mrs. Timmers went on. "Now you have to decide something, Alex. Do you want to be a visitor in my class, who gets special treatment, or do you want to be *in* my class?"

Alex looked at his hands. He had a bandage on his arm at the elbow. I guess the doctors had given him medicine through a needle yesterday.

"In the class," Alex said.

"Good. If you're in the class, then this thing is *out* of the contest. You boys may write another poem if you like."

During lunch, Alex and I wrote a poem about a jaguar. It was pretty good, and Mrs. Timmers let us turn it in. Later on, during Social Studies, Alex got up and went over to sharpen his pencil. He started grinding the sharpener like a sawmill while Mrs. Timmers was talking about Indian burial mounds. She stopped in the middle of a sentence.

"Alex, what are you doing?"

"My pencil's dull."

"Sit down, young man," she said.

Alex sat down.

Two weeks later, Martha won first prize in the contest for her poem about her messy room. Alex and I got honorable mention, but Martha got the twenty dollars.

For the school carnival at Halloween, Alex and I volunteered to run the duck-shooting booth. We stayed in at recess all week to make the booth. We even forgot to bug Louise.

On the day of the carnival, I crouched down behind the painted "lake." I bobbed the ducks across while the kids threw rubber-tipped darts. Alex stood in front and pushed tickets.

Our booth made the most money! That's because Alex knew how to get little kids to take another shot. He had a thousand ways to talk them into it.

"Hey," he'd say, "I know you can do better. I saw you jiggle the dart a little, but hold it steady, and you'll win!" The kid would plunk down another quarter. When a kid hit a duck, the prize was a little rubber duckie that said *quack.* Twenty kids wound up with little rubber duckies, and *we* wound up with $57.50 to give to the school library.

Nearby, Louise and Jane had a face-painting booth. When I saw Louise's face painted with purple-and-black goo, I told her she looked a lot better. It took so long to paint each face that the girls only made $13.75. Hah.

In November, I had my birthday party. Mom said I could have pizza and a sleepover for four friends. I chose Jeremy, Frank, Roger, and Alex. We stayed up most of the night telling stories and riddles and having pillow fights. It was my best birthday so far.

Alex said that if everything's okay, he'll invite us to sleep over on his birthday, in April.

"Yeah!" we all said.

Around three in the morning, Frank, Jeremy, and Roger were sleeping, but I was thinking. *Ten, ten, ten.* I kept saying it to myself to see if it really did sound better than *nine*. I wondered how old I might live to be. My great-grandpa is ninety! The stars were out, but the moon was sliding behind some clouds. I was pretty sure Alex was also awake because he kept wiggling his feet.

"Alex," I asked softly, "is this the latest you were ever awake?"

"Once I got up at three o'clock to go fishing."

"I was up all night once last year with the flu," I said.

"I got the flu last year, too," said Alex. "It took me three months to get over it, but I finally did."

We talked about whether three o'clock is late or early, and what time morning really is. Alex said astronomers can tell the exact time from the positions of the stars.

"Are you scared about AIDS, Alex?" I whispered into the dark.

"Yeah, sometimes," he said. "It makes me mad, too."

"I'm glad you sit next to me," I said. "I can help out when you miss school."

"I'm glad, too," he said. We finally fell asleep.

In December, there was ice and snow. One afternoon, our janitors, Pete and Ray, used hoses to flood the playground. We had a skating rink!

The next day, I was trying a double figure eight when I slipped and skidded along the ice. My skate sliced Alex's leg. It started to bleed.

In about one second the whole class gathered around in a circle. Nurses and teachers always think kids are babies and can't handle an emergency. But I was great. I took my mitten, turned it inside out to the clean part, and gave it to Alex to hold over his cut.

Louise knelt on the ice. "Don't worry, Alex," she said. "It's okay." She ran to get Mrs. Timmers. Mrs. Timmers put on rubber gloves from her first-aid kit. Using water from the fountain, she washed the cut, then put on antiseptic and bandaged Alex's leg.

"Everything's fine now," she said. It was no big scratch and no big deal.

"Do you think I'll make the papers?" asked Alex.

"I doubt it. Too bad, Jerk," I kidded him.

Alex laughed.

Today at recess we found a big, sleepy frog in a snowy clump of grass by the ditch. We named him Big Legs. We boys tried to corner him, but he slithered into the cattails.

"Can't you dummies catch a frog who's half-asleep?" Louise asked. She took her scarf and bagged him on the first try.

Alex doesn't get special favors anymore. Still, we decided he should be the one to ask Mrs. Timmers if we can keep Big Legs in our room. Alex can think of all the good educational reasons, and she'll probably say yes. I helped him zip the muddy frog into his jacket. Big Legs squirmed at first, but then he liked being where it was warm.

When summer comes, we'll let Big Legs go. Alex says we should have a goodbye ceremony out by the marsh and make a collar for Big Legs in case he ever comes back.

I hope in summer Alex will be here.